ABOUT THE NOK CREATORS

Donna Terjesen (Author) is a certified holistic counselor and founder of Nourish Our Kids, Inc.™ (NOK). Her experiences as a mother of three young daughters, her background in nutritional education and her recovery from a diagnosis of Multiple Sclerosis in 1992 were the catalysts that led her to create Nourish Our Kids, Inc.™ in 2003. Donna has worked vigilantly and tirelessly in her local community's nonprofit organizations and local government initiatives to support change and enhance nutritional education. She is committed to developing philosophies and products that integrate the NOK brand in every young child's school and home to creatively teach them and their parents about living a healthy and enriched life.

Angela Pariselli Velez (Author) joined Nourish Our Kids, Inc.™ in 2004 to support the company's goals in marketing, branding, product development, finances, and outreach efforts. As Angela has struggled with her own weight loss challenges due to a variety of life events and personal stresses, she is strongly committed to the company's goals in ending childhood obesity. In continuing her journey to adopt a more balanced and natural lifestyle, she wants to empower and inspire overweight parents to follow similar lifestyle philosophies.

Mark Biddison (Illustrator) had an early love of comic books and monster movies that ignited his passion for art and drawing. Illustrating a children's book has always been one of Mark's lifetime goals. Mark has worked in all phases of commercial art for the past twenty years including freelance illustration, graphic design, fashion drawing, and visual merchandising. As a father, he has a personal connection with the mission of Nourish Our Kids, Inc.™ to teach health and wellness to kids since one of his sons lives with the challenges of autism.

To learn more about Nourish Our Kids, Inc.™ and the company's educational and healthy products, go to
www.nourishourkids.com

THE NOK ROCKERS
TROUBLE IN
Slowville

Written by Nourish Our Kids, Inc.™
Illustrated by Mark C. Biddison

Acknowledgements

We need to recognize so many kindred spirits, friends, and family members who
have blessed us with their love, encouragement and support. Special thanks to our
dearly departed friend and angel, Al DeRosa. Extra special thanks to our angel on earth, Emily Komlossy.
Thanks and hugs to Judi Miller, for offering us her creative writing and joyful spirit. Deep gratitude to our
dear friend, Kit Wong.

Angela thanks her wonderful husband, Charlie - you always stand strong beside me, believing in my work
and encouraging me no matter what: I love you with all my heart.

Donna gives heartfelt thanks to her three girls, Lindsay, Kelly, and Jaimie - being your mother has profoundly
touched my heart; your unconditional love fills me with beams of light. Thank you for being my role models.
To my amazing husband Al - we share one heart and one soul, you complete me: I am blessed to receive your
endless patience, encouragement, and love.

To all those who are not mentioned here and have touched our hearts -
you know who you are - we thank you!

First Edition, Published by Nourish Our Kids, Inc.™
Copyright © 2011 by Nourish Our Kids, Inc.™
Nourish Our Kids, Inc.™, Saranna, James, Isaiah, and associated logos are registered trademarks of
Nourish Our Kids, Inc.™
All rights reserved.
No part of this book may be reproduced in any form or by electronic or mechanical means,
including information storage and retrievals systems, without written permission from the
copyright holder.
Printed in the United States
ISBN: 978-0-9848221-0-2

Isaiah and James were playing with a new train set when the pouring rain gave way to bright and welcome sunshine. Suddenly, Saranna burst through the door and shouted, "Boys, come outside! You won't believe this!"

Outside their door was the biggest and brightest rainbow they had ever seen. "Wait a second; that's not a real rainbow," said James.

Always the investigator, Isaiah whipped out his Discovery Pod, and James began juggling his favorite fruit to steady his nerves. Then, Saranna's special medallion began to glow.

The NOK Rockers smiled knowingly just before they spotted their special friend, Zoe, flipping and twirling over the rainbow.

She landed in front of them with one last double backflip. "You always make an exciting entrance," James cheered.

"Are you feeling OK?" asked Isaiah. "Your color is off." Her beautiful red hair and emerald eyes were now dim. "I'm OK, but I know some sad and sleepy people who only eat Junky Slow Foods like soda and candy and don't know that Go Foods like fruits and vegetables will make them happy and energetic," answered Zoe. "Does that mean another NOK Rockers adventure?" Isaiah asked. Zoe nodded.

With a snap of her fingers, Zoe transformed Isaiah's toy train into a life-sized locomotive. "Together, we will undo the colorless spell cast by the town bully, Junk Food Jammer."

GET READY NOK ROCKERS!

James whipped out his Rockin' Wireless Berry Blaster, Isaiah grabbed his Supertechie Discovery Pod, Saranna rolled up her yoga mat, and they excitedly boarded the train.

"Hurry now, you have a lot of work ahead of you! And remember, only you can break the Junk Food Jammer's spell." "But what about you?" Saranna asked sadly. "Oh, don't worry about me," said Zoe. "I will appear when you need me."

Immediately after climbing into the NOK Express, they heard a loud voice crackling through the speakers. "First stop, Slowville; second stop, anywhere else!"

"Here we go!" Isaiah said excitedly as the train sped off. James passed around snacks of chopped walnuts and sliced apples. "Adventures always make me hungry," he chuckled. "And these Go Foods are tasty!" Saranna and Isaiah agreed.

Suddenly, their eyes grew as huge as purple grapes as they caught sight of something outside their window. It was a grimy welcome sign. Saranna read it in a whisper,

"Welcome to Slowville... population declining..."

The NOK Express chugged along as if it were running out of fuel.
It huffed and puffed until it finally pulled into Slowville station.
Again, they heard the creepy voice as it echoed,

"You have arrived at your destination. Now, GET OUT!"

The NOK Rockers leapt out of the train into what looked like an old-fashioned, black and white movie. Everything was in shades of gray. "This looks like a cartoon strip," said Saranna. "Yeah," James agreed. "There is definitely something wrong here."

The three friends watched in dismay as a boy wolfed down a gigantic chunk of gooey chocolate cake, while a girl bought a bunch of french fries dripping with gooey cheese.

"Zoe is right. This town really needs our help," said Isaiah. "Look over there. I bet the Junk Food Jammer is in there!" shouted Saranna. James read the sign aloud,

"THE GREASY SPOON DINER-
ALL YOU CAN EAT. OPEN 24 HOURS."

The grumpy man was startled by the three colorful NOK Rockers.
"You kids hurt my eyes," he grumbled.
"Who are you?" Saranna asked boldly, her knees shaking.
Me?" he bellowed. "Who are you?!"...

"We asked you first," Isaiah answered. "They call me Junk Food Jammer!" he shouted. "I suppose you want to hear my story," said Junk Food Jammer, as he bit into his greasy burger. "Not exactly..." Isaiah bravely stated while James clapped his hand over Isaiah's mouth.

"One day I found a guitar at a local fair and discovered that

I had magical powers. When I play my slow songs,

it casts a spell over everyone. And NO ONE in Slowville

has the energy to stop me! I rule this town!"

"I can change a sack of potatoes into barrels of fries and

good healthy meats into fatty ones. Fruits become

mountains of sugary sweets. And veggies? Forget it.

I always throw them out. So don't bother me anymore!

I want everyone to stay the same

as me forever."

Then, Junk Food Jammer reached for his guitar and said, "Now I'm going to cast my Junk Food spell on you!" He began to play a slow, dreamy tune that made the NOK Rockers feel dizzy.

town so fast that the townspeople were amazed. They couldn't remember the last time they saw anyone with so much energy and color.

Running out of breath, they collapsed in front of an enormous brick wall.
They were shocked by all the graffiti scribbled on the wall in big bold letters.
"Now what do we do?" sighed Saranna.

All at once, James's Berry Blaster began to beep, Isaiah's Discovery Pod started to spin, and Saranna's NOK Rockers Medallion began to glow when the letter "J" popped out of the wall, jumped forward, and collapsed to the ground.

Cautiously, they crept through the hole to the other side. "Why, it's a garden!" Saranna said cheerfully. There were bushels of apples and pears and loads of raspberries, bananas, sweet corn, ripe cucumbers, spinach, cherries, and grapes. "Junk Food Jammer must have built that wall to keep all of these great Go Foods from the people of Slowville," said Isaiah.

The NOK Rockers ate heartily and drank water from the cool refreshing stream that ran through the garden.

Unexpectedly, Saranna jumped up and declared, "I know our mission! We have to teach the children of Slowville that they can feel happy again and have lots of energy if they choose Go Foods instead of eating the Junky Slow Foods that Jammer's spell makes them want to eat."

"And the best way to teach them is to show them," added Isaiah. "If only we still had the NOK Express, we could use it to carry these delicious Go Foods back to Slowville."

"So how do we get these foods back to Slowville?" Saranna wondered.

Once again, James's Berry Blaster began to beep, Isaiah's Discovery Pod started to spin, and Saranna's NOK Rockers Medallion began to glow. This time, Zoe appeared and swooped out of the sky riding on the NOK Express. "NOK Rockers, it sounds like you have a great plan. Let's get to work!" she declared.

Together, they loaded the wheelbarrows and bushels until they were full of fruits and vegetables. It seemed like it took only minutes before the NOK Express transformed into a beautiful rainbow of delicious Go Foods.

The NOK Rockers shouted "Let's Rock!" as they watched the NOK Express burst through Jammer's brick wall. They were excited to speed into town and build their Go Foods stand with delicious raspberries, blueberries, carrots, red peppers, cherries, broccoli, and watermelon for the kids to eat as their after school snack.

When the Slowville kids managed to chug and lumber out, the
NOK Rockers began passing out free Go Foods to everyone.
Isaiah gave a handful of red grapes to one girl.
"Yum!" she said and her hair turned red on the spot.

Saranna gave a tomato to a boy, who was suspicious at first, but when he tasted it, he grinned and his eyes turned bright green like Zoe's.

Seeing everyone's colorful transformation, Junk Food Jammer jumped up on the bandstand across from the NOK Rockers and growled, "I won't stand for this." He was amazed when the kids stood strong and began chanting. "We want to change! We want Go Foods! We choose Go Foods! We choose the NOK Rockers!"

"This is a trick. These colorful foods won't help you! I say NO to Go Foods,"
shouted back Jammer. "Listen to what the kids want," said Zoe. "They
haven't been tricked, Jammer. Why don't you see for yourself by
tasting a piece of this sweet fruit?"

As soon as Jammer swallowed his first bite, his appearance began to magically change and he looked younger, healthier, and happier.

The NOK Rockers leapt on stage and were thrilled to witness the healthy changes that were taking place in Slowville. "He needs a new name," said Isaiah to the other NOK Rockers and the children surrounding them. "How about Jammin' Jake?" yelled James. A roar of approval came from the crowd. With his shiny new guitar, Jammin' Jake and the NOK Rockers started playing the NOK Rockers theme song.

As the NOK Rockers peered around at the colorful and happy town, they all agreed their adventure was complete. They climbed aboard the NOK Express and waved farewell to Zoe, who was riding over the rainbow and applauding them. Lastly, Zoe changed the old Slowville welcome sign to: Goville Population...Growing Stronger!

THE NOK ROCKERS
THEME SONG

There's a rainbow over our house
Hey, now that's a sign
It's NOK Rockers' time
Here she comes, our cool friend, Zoe
Showing us the way, to live life every day

Hey, you are what you eat, so kick up your feet!
And let your body grow!
NOK Rockers, NOK Rockers, NOK Rockers GO!

Calling James, Isaiah, Saranna
Three new super friends
Adventure never ends
Berry Blaster, Mat, Medallion
Check Discovery Pod
Yeah, we're off with a nod

Oh, you are what you eat, so kick up your feet!
And let your body grow!
NOK Rockers, NOK Rockers, NOK Rockers GO!

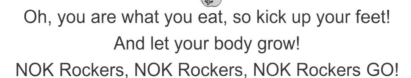

STAY TUNED FOR ANOTHER

NOK ROCKERS

ADVENTURE!